To Mum and Dad
– for the love of language and reading – M.N.

To Olivia – M.P.

Kelpies is an imprint of Floris Books
First published in 2017 by Floris Books

The publisher acknowledges subsidy from
Creative Scotland towards the publication
of this volume

MIX
Paper from
responsible sources
FSC® C117931

 Also available as an eBook

British Library CIP data available
ISBN 978-178250-363-7
Printed & bound by MBM Print SCS Ltd, Glasgow

and the Case of the
Curious Coins

Written by Mike Nicholson
Illustrated by Mike Phillips

Magda Gaskar

Gus

AND FEATURING...

Zoe Matsuo

Don the roofer

Some people think that museums are boring places.

Glass cases. Old stuff. Dust.

Wrong.

Think more of

wild animals

ANCIENT MUMMIES

enormous insects

COLOURFUL COSTUMES

glittering treasure

and amazing objects found nowhere else in the world.

Then imagine that each thing in the museum has its own strange story. With secrets from the past to be uncovered. Codes to be cracked. Odd characters and their fiendish plans. Each one creating a job for a team of expert investigators:

MUSEUM MYSTERY SQUAD

In this book you will find the Squad in the depths of the museum, somewhere in a maze of corridors and stairs.

Today, like every day, they have a puzzle to solve...

COLLECT THE COINS!

If Kennedy, Laurie and Nabster picked up all the 1p coins in their paths, who would have the correct change to buy Colin a bunch of carrots?

LAURIE

KENNEDY

NABSTER

Answer at the back

Chapter 1
In which there are inventions, robots and a possible thief

"Nearly there. Nearly there."

Nabster was concentrating hard. He was using a screwdriver to make a final adjustment to his latest invention.

The sound of heavy breathing wafted from the sofa. Laurie Lennox was in his usual place: almost invisible in his sleeping bag and almost unconscious. Beside the sofa stood his wardrobe rail with its vast selection of clothes and costumes. It was impossible to see which strange outfit Laurie had on today: in the sleeping bag he looked like a cross between a long cushion and a slug.

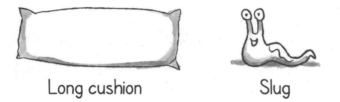

Long cushion   Slug

There was a third person in the hidden headquarters – a room deep under the museum, tucked away down many stairs and along a confusing number of corridors. This person was quiet, like Laurie, but *un*like Laurie she was very much awake. Kennedy Kerr had put her diary to one side and for once was focused on numbers, not words. Her jar of coins, which she had been filling for months, possibly *years*, had reached bursting point. Now as she sat in the Museum Mystery Squad's headquarters,

Kennedy was carefully counting the contents, stacking coins in neat piles. She was nearly finished, and was frowning from thinking so hard.

"There. That's it," said Nabster, putting down the screwdriver. "Now let's try it out." Mohammed McNab, or Nabster, was the Museum Mystery Squad's technical expert. In the Squad headquarters, you would usually find him on the laptop searching for information which then appeared on the giant smartboard screen. If he wasn't doing that he'd be making the team a hot chocolate with the voice-activated drinks machine he'd created, or screwing things together, or taking the same things apart again, or wondering whether these things might be better with a light, or a motor, or a helicopter rotor blade attached to them...

To use the technical phrase, he was always fiddling about with stuff.

Nabster proudly carried his new device to a small cage in the HQ. As he approached, a tiny nose appeared from a heap of straw. It was Colin, the Museum Mystery Squad's hamster.

Colin was cute. Colin was furry. And often without realising it, Colin helped the team solve cases by thinking in a different way. If he could speak, he would probably say, "Without me, there wouldn't even be a Museum Mystery Squad!" (However if Colin ever did utter even one word, he'd be whisked upstairs to the museum and put on display, because a talking hamster would be the freakiest exhibit EVER.)

"Right, my friend," said Nabster. "Let's see what you make of this."

Colin was about to receive a new toy.

"**SHHH!**" Kennedy was sweeping together the last uncounted coins. "I'm nearly there."

Nabster opened the cage door and, reaching in, carefully placed his invention inside.

Colin sniffed around it. He looked uncertain about this new piece of equipment in his home. He sniffed some more. He seemed to be thinking, "I don't remember ordering this."

Then, catching a whiff of something *all* hamsters love to eat, his sniffs turned into deliberate nose-pokes.

There were four coloured buttons on the device. Red, blue, green and yellow. Each one did something different:

- the red one turned on a light,
- the blue one chimed a bell,
- the green one spun a wheel,
- and last but *definitely* not least, the yellow one popped out a tray with a little piece of carrot on it.

16

"The world's first multi-sensory hamster

amusement device!" announced Nabster grandly.

"SSSSHHHH!" said Kennedy again.

"We'd better be quiet," said Laurie to Nabster. "She must be about to reach double figures."

Kennedy glared at him from behind her coin towers.

Somehow, although he appeared to be asleep, Laurie always knew what was going on. "Maybe you could make *me* something now," he said to Nabster. "Like a machine that fluffs up my cushions."

"If I did that, you'd never move at all," said Nabster, "since cushion-fluffing is pretty much your only daily exercise."

"How about inventing something which can tell you how many coins are in a jar," said Kennedy, who had finally finished counting.

"I could do *that* for you," said Nabster, "as long as

I got to keep half the cash at the end." He was now back at his seat and tapping on the laptop. "Mind you, if we go upstairs you might find a machine that would do it for free. Look."

Filling the smartboard screen was an ad for a new robot exhibition at the museum, showing a robot with a white head, disc-shaped eyes and a quirky mouth:

New Exhibition!

The Robot Next Door

Meet an outstanding collection of the hyper-intelligent robots that will become part of everyday life in our future homes.

"Looks great," said Laurie. "There's bound to be one that can count. What did your coins add up to, anyway?"

Kennedy was sweeping the money back into her jar. There was a pause.

She scrunched up her eyes to remember... Then she buried her head in her hands and groaned: "Nooooo!"

"You haven't forgotten, have you?" Laurie grinned.

Kennedy's face reddened, almost matching her frizzy hair. "I didn't write it down! All your chat distracted me!"

Nabster looked a little guilty. "Maybe we *should* go upstairs and look for a counting robot," he said.

Laurie sat up and stretched. "Sounds like a plan. Now, what would be the best outfit to wear to a robot exhibition? Hmm..." He considered a few possibilities before picking out a silver shirt with a metallic sheen, and a large pair of yellow headphones. With his big glasses on too, he looked as if he had a robot's head. Somehow the overall effect was still good – just Laurie Lennox being himself.

Kennedy stared at her jar and sighed.

The sound of an email appearing in the laptop inbox was the perfect way to cheer her up. The Squad often found out about a new mystery by email.

Sure enough, the new message was from Museum
Director Magda Gaskar and it was asking for their help.

To: **MMS@museums.co.uk**
Subject: Investigation required

Dear Kennedy, Laurence and Mohammed,
I trust you are all well? I have a new job for you.
Something strange is happening with money donated
by visitors. We might have a thief – a clumsy one!
   Let me explain...

Chapter 2
In which a tiny key is revealed

Nabster displayed Magda's email on the smartboard screen for the three Squad members to read:

> As you know there is a large container near the museum's front door where visitors donate money. There were some coins lying on the floor beside it when the cleaners arrived yesterday morning, and again today. These coins were *definitely* not there when the museum was locked up at closing time the day before. Very odd.

Someone has been up to something. But we don't know who or what.

Please can you look into this for me?

Kind regards,

Magda Gaskar

Museum Director

"That's weird," said Kennedy. "Where are the coins coming from? From inside the container? Is someone getting into the museum at night?"

"If someone was taking coins out," asked Laurie, "why would they leave them scattered on the floor?" Laurie had a special talent for asking the questions everyone else was thinking.

"Maybe they're just not bothered about the coins," said Nabster. "If I was a thief I'd choose banknotes rather than coins. They're worth more and they're quieter! Has any paper money gone missing?"

"Good question. We'd better examine this donations container." Kennedy was already heading to the door. Laurie was right behind her; in his outfit he looked like a robot made of shiny melted 5p pieces.

"Can we still visit the robot exhibition while we're up there?" asked Nabster hopefully. The Squad's inventor was thinking that a room full of robots sounded more exciting than spare change scattered on the floor.

"We'd better check out Magda's mystery first," said Kennedy firmly.

Nabster grumbled but began packing what he'd need for an investigation:

this notebook, pen

camera

solar-powered pencil sharpener

electronic measuring tape

random bits of wire and pliers

packet of mints (soft)

packet of mints (hard)

rubber bands (collected from the pavement)

scribbled list of possible inventions to create

packet of hot-chocolate powder

spare sock (one)

carrot (belonging to Colin)

the ScanRay (best-ever gadget!)

The ScanRay was often a great help to the Squad in tricky cases. It could tell what any object was made from. If you pointed it at a cake, it would tell you the ingredients (although eating cake and guessing the ingredients is more fun).

Hmmm... I think raspberries... I'll try another bite.

Looking up, Nabster realised he was on his own. Kennedy had charged off as usual – as well as being super-smart, she was super-speedy. And Laurie had quickly followed her.

Nabster grabbed his bag and ran after them.

Colin was all alone, but he didn't mind. He had worked out what the yellow button did on his new machine and was happily pressing it and munching on the results.

Up in the museum entrance hall, there wasn't really a lot to see. The container looked like... a container. No surprise there. This particular container was big and made of thick, clear plastic. It had a slot in the top large enough for coins and notes to fit through, but far too narrow for even a child's hand to squeeze in. There was then a drop before the money hit the bottom.

"Hey, Kennedy, how many coins do you reckon it would take to fill something that size?" asked Nabster.

Kennedy made a face that said she didn't want to think about counting money again for now.

Nabster pulled out his electronic measuring tape and checked the size of the slot (8 cm across and 1.5 cm wide) and the distance from the slot to the bottom of the container (40 cm). "It's obvious how money gets in

28

there, but I can't see how anyone could get it out again," he said, standing back.

"It would be easy if you had the key for that little door." Kennedy pointed to a small panel with a keyhole.

Laurie took off his headphones and bent down to look. "So the first question is: Who has the key?"

"I do," said a voice behind them.

Of course. It was the one person you would expect to have the key: Gus the security guard.

Gus was a good friend to the Squad. He had often helped them in solving cases, and was usually only a walkie-talkie call away.

Pulling his navy jacket to one side, Gus revealed a chain attached to his belt that had about twenty keys on it.

He flicked through them as though he knew what each one was for, until he reached the smallest.

"This," he said, brandishing the tiny key, "is the only thing which can open that container. It's so clever I call it Sherlock! Get it? Clever and a key? Sherlock? Sher-LOCK?"

The only downside to working with Gus was that he liked making jokes that weren't very funny. Not funny at all. His favourite joke was: 'What is brown and sticky?' The answer was: 'a stick'. Nobody else thought this was funny. Gus found it very funny indeed.

The team watched as he bent down and inserted the key into the little door. It sprang open.

"Are you the only one with a key?" asked Laurie.

Gus nodded.

Laurie continued: "And are your keys always attached to you?"

Gus nodded again.

With Laurie asking questions, in two minutes the team knew the following facts:

- Visitor numbers = normal in recent days.

- Donations container stand is fixed to the floor. Container can't be lifted or turned upside down.

- Yesterday + today some 1p, 2p, 5p and 10p coins scattered around the container in the morning when museum opened.

- No banknotes on the floor, only coins.

- Some coins and banknotes still left in container.

- Can't tell if any money has gone missing, because total donated amounts = different each day and container is only emptied for counting every few weeks.

- Gus carries only key.

"Ah good. I'm glad you're already here." It was Magda Gaskar, the museum director, passing by on her way to a meeting. "Someone must have been meddling with this money but we don't know who or how or why. It's odd – I'd like to get to the bottom of it. We have to be careful with security at the museum, as so many of our objects are valuable – much more valuable than a few coins."

She had just finished speaking when the entrance hall filled with a loud buzz of voices. A group of school children were gathering at the end of their museum visit. "Let me know if you find anything," Magda said, and continued on her way. Gus followed, carrying on with his rounds.

The Squad let the chattering children pass by before discussing their next steps. But while they were talking together, a coin theft began right in front of their eyes.

Chapter 3
In which a new use is found for something sticky

The school group was milling around, waiting a few minutes before catching their bus.

It was Kennedy who spotted something odd in the busy scene. "Keep an eye over there," she muttered softly. "Look at those two."

A girl and a boy were leaning on the top of the donations container, peering in at the pile of coins. From the way they were pointing, it looked like they were trying to add up what was inside. They seemed quite excited about the total.

"What a cheek! I think they're trying to work out how to get at the money!" whispered Nabster. The boy was demonstrating the distance between the slot in the top of the container and the cash. He glanced around to see if anyone was watching. The rest of the school children were talking in little groups or peering at display cases in the entrance area. With no one paying attention to them, the boy and girl seemed invisible in the thick of the crowd.

The Museum Mystery Squad also appeared to be a little group casually chatting. But all their concentration was on the two school children.

The boy pulled a ruler out of his bag and looked around again before testing whether it fitted through the slot in the top of the container.

It did.

Holding the ruler with the very tips of his fingers he lowered it towards the money until his hand hit the top of the container and could go no further. The girl grinned, said something and reached into her bag.

"What's she doing?" asked Laurie. The girl fiddled with a small packet and popped something in her mouth. It seemed to be part of a plan.

"I get it," said Kennedy. "They've worked out that the ruler reaches the coins, but can't pick one up."

"So what's the answer?" asked Laurie, still trying to figure out how eating could help.

"Chewing gum," replied Kennedy.

Nabster smiled the approving smile of an inventor. "That's pretty smart actually. And a bit gross."

Sure enough, the girl took a wad of freshly chewed chewing gum out of her mouth and stuck it around one end of the ruler, making it flat so it would still fit through the coin slot. They were one step closer to removing a coin.

Poking Coins

Stealing Coins

"Get Gus!" said Nabster. "They're about to nick something!"

"No need," said Kennedy. "They're busted."

Approaching fast was a teacher with a determined stride and a very cross expression on her face.

"Christopher Scott! WHAT do you think you are doing?"

"It was her idea, miss," the boy said, pointing at the girl. That comment marked a sudden end to the friendship of these partners in crime.

"I was only joking," retorted the girl. "It was *you* who actually did it." She looked disgusted with the boy as she folded her arms in fury.

"Well it's *your* chewing gum!" said the boy.

"It's *your* ruler," said the girl.

"And it's the last time *you two* are going on any school trips," said the teacher, confiscating the ruler. Unfortunately she grabbed the end with the chewing gum, which stuck to her hand. The boy laughed, then stopped when he realised that the teacher was now doubly cross. She marched them away to the museum exit.

"I bet they'll have to sit beside her on the bus home," said Laurie, smiling.

"It was quite clever really," said Nabster. "She should give them a bit of praise for their ingenious invention! Do you think that's how coins ended up on the floor overnight?"

"Pulled out using something sticky?" wondered Kennedy. "Like sellotape or glue..."

"Or just a magnet," said Laurie casually.

They all looked at each other. Was that possible?

A magnet?

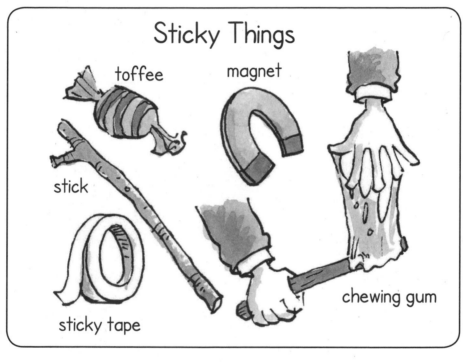

Sticky Things

toffee

magnet

stick

sticky tape

chewing gum

Back in the Squad headquarters, Kennedy set out a row of different coins on the table: 1p, 2p, 5p, 10p, 20p, 50p, £1 and £2.

Meanwhile Nabster rummaged in a cupboard. "Got one!" he said, pulling out a magnet. He tossed it to Laurie, who moved it slowly above the coins.

Click! – the 1p flew up and stuck to the magnet.
Click! – the 2p did the same.
Click! – then the 5p.
Click! – 10p.

Then... nothing. The other coins didn't move a millimetre.

"It's stopped working," said Laurie, looking doubtfully at the magnet, confused by the coins that were still stuck to it. "How is that possible? I thought all metal was magnetic. Are some of these coins fake?"

"If I remember correctly," said Nabster, "coins are made of different kinds of metal." He reached into his bag and pulled out the ScanRay.

He pressed a switch and it began to hum. Within a minute he had found that the coins sticking to the magnet all had steel in them – steel, made from iron.

The coins that hadn't moved were made of:

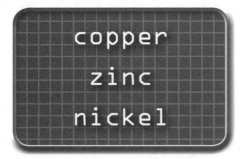

copper

zinc

nickel

"Does that explain why some coins could be removed from the container and some were left behind?"

"We could check whether all the coins that ended up on the floor are magnetic. That would tell us how they might have got there."

"But wait, even if that is what's happening, why?"

"Yeah. What's the point of taking coins out and leaving them on the floor?"

They all looked blank. The magnet had seemed like a breakthrough, but the most important questions were still unanswered.

"We need more information. If we could spy on the donations container at night we could see what was going on," said Nabster.

"But there's nowhere for us to hide in the entrance hall," said Laurie. "And the security cameras only watch the main doors. We need a special hidden camera."

"Wait," said Kennedy. "That's it. With the new exhibition, this building is full of robots designed to be helpful. Maybe there's one that could help us watch the entrance hall tonight."

"I knew it was a good idea to go and see the robots," said Nabster happily.

45

WHAT'S THE POINT OF MAGNETS?

We use magnets to stick notes to the fridge, but they're far more important than that! Here are some of the other ways people use magnets.

JUNKYARD

Giant magnets (electromagnets) are used in junkyards to lift up cars and sort metal for recycling.

MAGLEV TRAIN

'Maglev' is short for magnetic levitation. These trains hover above the track using magnets. They can travel at more than 600 km per hour! If you want to travel on one, you'll need to go to Japan, South Korea or China!

COMPASS

The Earth is a bit like a giant magnet. The magnet inside a compass is attracted to the Earth's magnetic field, which helps us find North. We'd be lost without magnets!

TRY IT AT HOME

What happens when you put a magnet next to a compass?

TRY IT AT HOME

Put a piece of paper in the bottom of a shoe box. Drip a few spots of paint on it and drop in a paperclip. Then move a magnet around underneath the box to make a magnet painting!

COMPUTERS

Billions of tiny magnetic dots on a computer hard drive (each the width of a human hair) sense elecric current and, used together, can store information.

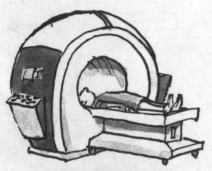

VENDING MACHINES

Magnets in vending machines help sort different coins to calculate how much you've paid. Even bank notes have magnetic ink.

MRI MACHINE

MRI (Magnetic Resonance Imaging) machines contain powerful magnets that can scan the magnetic field produced by each cell in our body to create a picture. This helps doctors see what's going on inside us!

Chapter 4
In which a strange
new voice is heard

As the Squad stepped through the doorway of
'The Robot Next Door' exhibition, a voice spoke.

"May I help you?"

It wasn't human.

"Please state how I can assist you."

Everyone turned to see a shiny white figure the
size of a small adult. Its head swivelled to look at them
all with two big round eyes over a short fixed comical
smile. It looked like a friendly Star Wars stormtrooper.

"Please state how I can assist you," it said again.

"Who are you?" asked Laurie.

"I am BigPal. I am here to help you," said the robot in a machine-like but polite way.

"Who's controlling you?" asked Laurie.

"I'm sorry but can you repeat the question?" asked the robot.

"I can answer that one," said another voice. "It's me." A smiling young woman with short dark spiky hair approached them, holding a remote-control handset.

"Is she like the Queen of Robots or something?" said Laurie quietly, taking in the woman's shiny steel-toe-capped boots and her dangling silver robot earrings.

The Queen of Robots introduced herself as Zoe Matsuo, the technician for the robot exhibition.

"I keep the show on the road. If anything breaks or malfunctions, I get to fix it."

"I think you might have my dream job," said Nabster, approaching BigPal the robot for a closer look.

BigPal responded by moving towards Nabster, slowly lifting an arm and putting out a hand. Each movement

happened because Zoe was adjusting the joystick on the remote control.

"Pleased to meet you," BigPal said. His white plastic eyelids blinked slowly over round staring eyes.

"That's so cool!" Nabster shook the robot's hand.

"We've just entered Nabster heaven," said Kennedy.

It was true. Nabster was already goggle-eyed and open-mouthed and they had only just got through the door. There were robots of every shape and size on display, a collection of shiny machines making short efficient movements. Some were programmed for particular jobs, some began working at pre-set times of day, others were voice-activated. "Beautiful... amazing... just... just perfect..." breathed Nabster.

There were robot arms that could build flat-pack furniture, robots that could give massages, others that could prepare and cook food. There were even robots like worms, which could go down a plughole and investigate why a drain was blocked. Museum visitors were pressing buttons, passing objects to robot arms and watching two robots assemble a toy aeroplane.

Wandering around them, Kennedy reminded the Squad that a robot which could operate a camera would really help their coin investigation. She added that she'd also like to find one that counted coins from a jar.

Back at the tech desk, Zoe was using a soldering iron on a circuit board. Her robot earrings sparkled as she worked. Nabster was torn between inspecting the displays and watching her fix things.

"What's that one?" asked Laurie. He pointed at a small white robot. It looked like an exact copy of BigPal but was a fraction of the size.

"Oh, that's WeePal," replied Zoe. "That was the prototype for the one you've met. They perfected the design on that size and then built the bigger one." She held out a remote control. "Want a go?"

Nabster gasped in excitement.

Zoe explained the controls and each Squad member had a shot.

Kennedy managed to make WeePal walk across the room, stop at a barrier, and then return. Laurie had a few more problems. He tried to get WeePal walking backwards but the little robot fell over and got stuck on his back – like a beetle with its legs in the air – and needed help to get on his feet again.

"He takes after you," said Nabster. "Flat out."

"The big difference, though, is WeePal is still moving," added Kennedy.

"Shame I can't switch you two off," replied Laurie, giving them his sweetest smile.

It was no surprise that Nabster was the quickest to get the robot moving with ease. He managed to make WeePal pick up a screwdriver from Zoe's kit, wave it in the air, then walk over and hand it to Zoe. She said a polite "Thank you," at which the robot bowed, then sprinted round the room in a lap of honour.

Zoe was impressed. "Ever thought of a career with robots?"

"Don't pinch him from us!" said Kennedy. "We need him in our team!"

"Aw. That's really nice of you." Nabster was touched by the comment.

"It's just that Laurie and I can't work the hot chocolate machine," Kennedy added.

Laurie shook his head and grinned. "You know, Colin could probably do most of what Nabster does."

"Or if we can't train Colin, perhaps a robot could replace Nabster?" said Kennedy.

"Oi! One minute you can't do without me, and the next you've ditched me for a machine," said Nabster. He wasn't really bothered by the banter. He was buzzing from being surrounded by so much impressive engineering.

At that moment the door opened and Gus appeared. At least it seemed to be Gus, but his arms and legs moved stiffly, like a machine.

"I-thought-you-lot-might-be-in-here," said the new Gus in a robot-style voice. **"I-am-BoGus, the-new-security-robot-that-walks-around-with-lots-of-keys-and-keeps-an-eye-on-things."**

Zoe smiled.

"This might actually be worse than one of his usual jokes," said Laurie quietly.

"Wait, look, it's just me pretending!" Gus shook his arms and legs to show he wasn't really a robot.

"You nearly had us there," Nabster lied, trying to sound like he meant it.

"Bogus. Get it? Bo-Gus. Fake. Bo-GUS?"

"Do you have a robot that can tell jokes?" Laurie asked Zoe. "Gus could buy one to help him!"

"WeePal is certainly helpful but he hasn't got much sense of humour," said Zoe.

"Sounds just like Gus," whispered Nabster.

"I reckon robot help would cost more than I can afford," said Gus. "I already know what I'm doing with my pay at the end of this month. I've been saving up to buy a new pair of these." He lifted one shoe off the ground, showing a hole worn in the bottom and a pink sock poking out. "I get through a lot of shoe leather in my job, and it's pricey," he said. "These have had their day. They're history. Maybe I should donate them to the museum! We could rename it the *shoe-seum*!"

Nobody laughed. As usual.

Kennedy took the chance to change the subject, explaining to Zoe that they were in search of a robot to help with some filming.

"It would be good to get the robots working for real," said Zoe. "Come back after closing time when I've finished up. We can have a think about which robot might be useful." The Squad exchanged cheerful glances. This was at least a little progress in their investigation.

Magda came in to ask Zoe how visitors were reacting to the robot exhibition. And she also questioned the Squad: "Any closer to cracking the coin conundrum?"

"Well..." Kennedy began. "Like any investigation..."

"We've had some good ideas that are worth *sticking* with," said Laurie.

"And we might have a better *picture* of what's happening by tomorrow," finished Nabster with a grin.

Before anyone could invent more Gus-like puns, something dropped from the sky.

Chapter 5
In which there is whizzing and buzzing and a claw

There was a high-pitched whizzing sound.

"Watch out below!"

WHIZZ BUZZZZZZZ

Magda and the Squad members glanced up. A figure was approaching fast from above. He seemed to fall in slow motion as he expertly abseiled to the ground. The journey from the museum's high ceiling to a safe landing had taken no more than five seconds. The man arrived on the floor beside a bag of tools and an area marked off with four cones and a {WORK IN PROGRESS} sign.

"We've had some problems with the roof," explained Magda. "We're getting it checked out and repaired."

"I wish it was as quick getting back up there," said the man. He removed the abseiling clip from his safety harness.

"How's the job going?" Magda asked him.

"Pretty well," the man replied. "Another day and you'll be watertight again."

"Perfect," said Magda. "We can't have rusty robots. We had to get Don here on the job in double-quick time when the roof sprang a leak."

Don nodded to everyone. The roofer had close-cropped red hair, a beard to match, and sparkly blue eyes.

"You must have a good head for heights," said Laurie, looking at the distance the man had dropped.

"I love being up high," said Don with a grin. "Always have done. Right from when I was a kid. I think I spent most of my childhood up a tree. Roof repair suits me perfectly!"

Nabster couldn't help admiring the amount of equipment Don was carrying. Or not so much carrying as *wearing*. He had a belt with all sorts of tools attached. Meanwhile his jacket had pockets in the usual places, but also extra ones on the arms and a pouch on the back. Nabster immediately began working out how he could organise his own kit in the same way. He could forget carting around a heavy bag if he just adapted some of his clothes!

It was Laurie who noticed one slightly unusual piece of equipment around the roofer's neck. "Why do you need binoculars to fix a roof?"

"You don't," said Don with a smile. "But when you're up there you get a great view of the city, and the chance to do a bit of birdwatching. Sometimes I put seeds out and have lots of feathered company!"

Don went off to buy a sandwich, and the Squad might have been thinking of lunch too, but Magda had a suggestion for them: "There's another new exhibition opening in the room next door in two days' time. It's already mostly set up, and it might be helpful while you are researching coins. It's called **Splash the Cash** and it's full of information about money."

"**Splash the Cash**?" said Kennedy. "If the roof's still leaking then that's exactly what might happen!"

"Hopefully not," said Magda. "Especially since one of the displays is worth a million pounds."

"A million pounds?" said Laurie. "Never mind robots – let's take a look at that!"

He and Kennedy persuaded Nabster to leave the robots for a while and explore the other exhibition.

"It's a journey through time and money," read Kennedy, as they walked past the introductory panels for the **Splash the Cash** exhibition. Inside, there were lots of examples of how people had made and spent money through the ages, with displays of Iron Age coins, Bronze Age coins, Roman coins, and other objects once used as payment, like shells and beads. An interactive screen let you brush virtual earth away from a coin, as if you were working at an archaeological dig. A series of faces looked out at them from the walls: famous people who had all appeared on coins and banknotes. Other parts of the room glittered with coins made from precious metals.

Laurie admired the sparkling silver currency, "Surely this is the exhibit that's worth a million?"

66

But there was no £1,000,000 price-tag to be seen.

"What about this?" asked Nabster. He pointed to a display case that had been designed to look like a fancy money box. It had glass sides, brass corners, and a brass plate on top with swirly engraving around a coin slot.

"Nah," said Laurie. "There's only one coin inside!" He peered in, leaning forward until his big glasses touched the side of the box. "This would be nice and easy for Kennedy to count," he said.

Kennedy gave him a withering glance through the glass, then looked closely at the information beside the display and stepped back in shock. "This IS it! One million pounds! How can one coin be worth that much?"

The Squad gathered round. Inside the box was a rather battered-looking gold coin with a very unusual feature. It had four pointed metal spikes gripping its edges.

"Claws?" asked Laurie. The coin had been made to look as though a bird or animal was clutching it.

"It's like the foot of an iron eagle," said Nabster.

Kennedy read aloud.

The Coin in the Claw dates from the early 1300s. It was cast to commemorate Robert the Bruce becoming King of the Scots, and is thought to have become the warrior's lucky charm.

"A famous king's cash!"

"Majestic money!"

"No wonder it's worth a lot. It's the only one in the world!"

"Can you imagine going into a shop for some sweets and trying to pay with that?" asked Nabster.

69

"You could buy the shop!" laughed Laurie.

They stared at the valuable coin before wandering through the rest of the **Splash the Cash** exhibition, but nothing helped them learn why coins might be scattered round a museum donations container.

Nabster stopped at a giant screen split into quarters. He stood in front of it, hypnotised. The film was of machinery rolling out new banknotes and each of the four quarters of the screen showed the process from a different angle. "This has given me an idea," he said. "I'll tell Zoe we don't want just one robot to help with filming. We want lots! That way we'll have different camera angles on the donations container and the entrance hall."

Kennedy and Laurie looked at the screen. They shrugged at each other, but Nabster had a familiar grin on his face – one that usually meant he had come up with a brilliant technical fix.

The Squad headed back to the HQ to wait until Zoe would be free to help them. Nabster's focus shifted to an entirely different invention. Instead of his usual wires and screwdriver, he picked up a needle and thread.

First he sewed a narrow pocket onto the arm of his hoodie. He tested it by sliding a pen in and out. Happy with this, he then found an old belt and designed holders to hang off it, along with various clips. He spent some time working out where each piece of his equipment would fit best: his walkie-talkie, the ScanRay and his camera.

Nabster had been inspired.

"I want to try carrying stuff the way that roofer, Don, does," he said. "He has everything so close to hand."

If Nabster was busy, Laurie was the opposite. He was fitting in a quick sofa snooze while things were quiet. Colin was sleepy too. His eyelids were drooping after a busy day pressing his new toy's yellow button.

Meanwhile, Kennedy was as lively as ever, scribbling away in her diary, turning over what they knew about the donation box coins.

Kennedy's Diary

Thursday, 4.00 p.m.
   Ok, so money is disappearing from the donations container overnight.
   Overnight.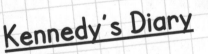

Who is in the building at night?

No one.
(Except Gus when he does a night shift.)
The container is locked, sealed, fixed to its
stand and the floor.
You could get money out with a magnet
(or chewing gum if you were lucky). Or you
can take it straight out of the little door.

What opens the door? <u>A key.</u>
Who has the key? Gus.
Who needs money at the moment? £££
Gus. For new shoes!!

So who is the Number 1 suspect?

? ?₂? (Gus) ?²₂?

Surely it can't be...

Chapter 6
In which cameras are put in place

"I can't believe I'm saying this but we need to keep an eye on Gus. A lot of the evidence points to him." Kennedy explained her line of thinking.

The others were shocked but had to agree.

Nabster came up with a plan. "It's nearly museum closing time, so Zoe should be ready to help us with robots and cameras. But let's find Gus on our way, just to check what he's doing."

Laurie felt reluctant to move but squirmed out of his sleeping bag.

Kennedy felt worried that they might be about to catch a friend up to no good.

Nabster felt happy because they were going to work with robots.

Colin felt content. He was warm and full of carrot pieces and still had other buttons to press on his new toy.

As it turned out, the Museum Mystery Squad found Gus chatting to Zoe at her tech desk in the robot exhibition. From a distance, the two of them appeared to be looking closely at something. The Squad slowed, so they wouldn't interrupt. Kennedy's eyes narrowed, watching as Gus counted out coins and Zoe looked on.

He reached into his pocket, and added more to the pile.

The Squad whispered to each other.

"What's he doing?"

"Where did he get all those coins?"

"Could they be from the donations container?"

"It must be tempting to take some if you have the key to it."

"Surely not?" protested Laurie, still whispering. "Gus... a thief?"

"There you go," they heard Gus say to Zoe. "Don't spend it all at once."

"Thanks so much," Zoe replied with a smile. "That's a big help."

Even though the Squad were still a few metres away, there was no doubting that Gus had just given Zoe a handful of coins.

The security guard turned as he heard footsteps approach, but gave no hint he had been doing anything wrong. "Hi you lot, how's it going?"

None of the team wanted to challenge their friend about what they had seen, but they also felt unable to chat normally.

"Something up?" asked Gus, looking at each of the three in turn. "You're acting funny. I thought I was the funny one!"

Kennedy, Nabster and Laurie couldn't help glancing at the pocket where the handful of change had been.

Gus's eyes narrowed as he thought. "Oh I get it," he said. "You've got me down as the coin thief, haven't you?"

The three looked nervously away.

"Well, you're quite right to think that," said Gus.

"Why? Is it really you?" Laurie was shocked.

"No!" said Gus. "Don't be daft! But it all points to me, doesn't it? In fact I'd be disappointed if the Museum Mystery Squad didn't consider me a suspect. But I can assure you it's not me. This is my own cash, and I was giving Zoe some change for her bus fare home!"

Zoe nodded. "It's true," she said.

Kennedy relaxed first. "Sorry, Gus. We knew that it couldn't really be you, but we're struggling to think who could get coins out – and why they'd want to."

"Maybe someone just dropped them and hasn't noticed," said Gus. "I lost some coins through a hole in my pocket once. I know you think I'm tall, but I was a bit short that day!" He grinned. "Short... Get it? Not tall? Short, as in short of money..."

The Squad members smiled weakly, but fortunately a noise from above distracted them all. It was Don, dangling high over them again, repairing a joint between glass panels in the roof. He waved cheerily and shouted hello.

"Hi!" Gus replied. "Get it? Hi... high!"

A high 'Hi!'

Nabster sighed and everyone else looked embarrassed.

"Will you be *hanging around* here for much longer?"
Gus craned his neck speaking to Don.

"No, I'm finishing up for today, and tomorrow's my
last morning – then the job will be done," the roofer
explained. "These robots can put away their umbrellas
after that."

"His jokes are nearly as bad as Gus's," muttered Laurie.

They watched Don zip to the ground, pack up, wave goodbye and head out with the last museum visitors. Gus had a night off and he left too.

The Squad still had an unsolved mystery, but they were glad to know Gus wasn't a thief. And they hoped the mystery might be solved that very night, now Zoe and her robots were going to help. In the museum entrance hall, Nabster enthusiastically described the split-screen display in the **Splash the Cash** exhibition to Zoe, who got the idea quickly and chose four different robots to film from different angles.

The drain-clearing worm robot had an in-built camera. Zoe asked Gus to open the donations container and she placed the worm robot inside, buried in the pile of money with the camera facing up. It could film the container's slot from underneath.

Already positioned in the entrance hall, promoting The Robot Next Door exhibition, were two big robotic arms, like the ones used to make cars. They formed an archway over a door near the donations container, and Zoe hid a small camera on each one.

There was also a job for WeePal. Zoe stood the little robot on a pedestal with his arm pointing to the exhibition. He looked like part of the promotion, but, with a tiny hidden camera on his shoulder, WeePal had a far more important job to do.

With the cameras in place, the Squad settled down for the night in the HQ. Nabster had arranged the big wall screen so each quarter showed the view from one of the four robot cameras. The Squad could watch the entrance hall from every position at once.

"I knew this would work!" Nabster was delighted that his idea was up and running.

"Live TV!" said Kennedy, as Zoe's face appeared in one quarter of the screen giving them a thumb's up.

"I love this idea," said Laurie. "We sit back, relax and watch what happens."

"That's no different to what you normally do," said Nabster, as he made sure the four images were sharp.

Zoe appeared again in the view from WeePal's camera, and waved goodbye, before turning away. The Squad saw her walk to the far end of the entrance hall, put on her coat, then step out of view.

Kennedy's Diary

Thursday, 7.00 p.m.

We're all organised. Last night and the night before, coins were scattered about.

Tonight will be different.

If any coins start doing curious things, we are ready.

WeePal, the robot arms and the robot worm will be filming whatever goes on, and we'll be watching...

For once it wasn't just Laurie on the sofa. Kennedy and Nabster were relaxing too. Nabster had made hot chocolates and popcorn.

"This is my kind of investigating," said Laurie. "Solving mysteries in comfort!"

But it wasn't that straightforward. Within twenty minutes the snacks and drinks were finished and signs of boredom were beginning to show.

"This is the worst film I've ever seen," complained Laurie.

"It's worse than that even. It's the worst *four* films I've ever seen," said Nabster. It was true. Nothing was happening in any quarter of the screen. There were just four unchanging views of the donations container, with its coins safely resting inside.

"We have to be patient," said Kennedy, but she was starting to fidget.

Ten minutes later they had all given up. Laurie had the sofa to himself again. His slow breathing indicated a deep sleep. Nabster was online, researching how to wire a robot's hand. Kennedy had her diary open, but she had nothing to report, so had been drawing a giant robot.

The screen still showed pictures from the four cameras but no one was paying any attention to them.

That meant that no one was watching when one of the images started to show something very surprising. Very surprising indeed. Something was moving, but it was the one thing that no one would have predicted.

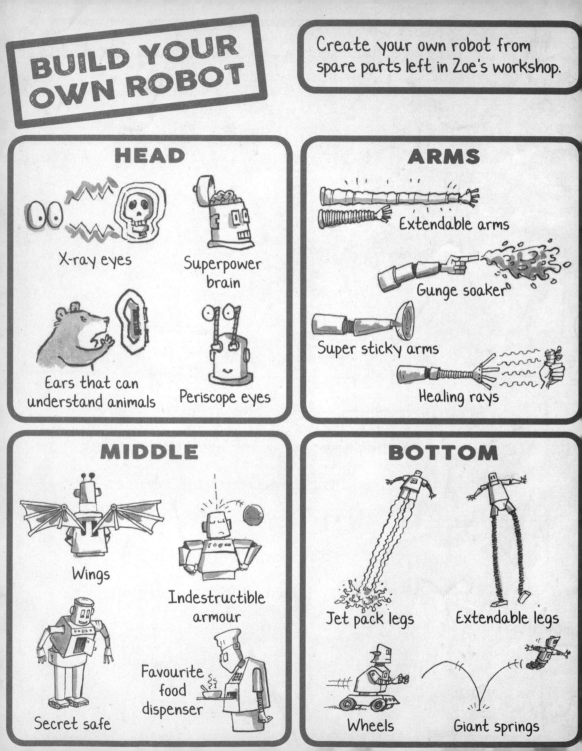

BUILD YOUR OWN ROBOT

Create your own robot from spare parts left in Zoe's workshop.

HEAD

X-ray eyes

Superpower brain

Ears that can understand animals

Periscope eyes

ARMS

Extendable arms

Gunge soaker

Super sticky arms

Healing rays

MIDDLE

Wings

Indestructible armour

Secret safe

Favourite food dispenser

BOTTOM

Jet pack legs

Extendable legs

Wheels

Giant springs

Choose one part from each section and draw your dream robot.
What can it do?

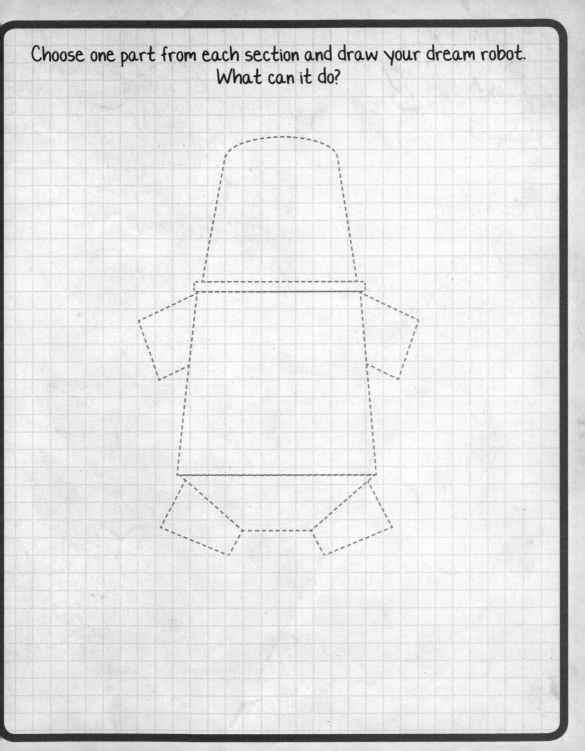

Chapter 7
In which WeePal takes a surprising change of direction

Laurie turned over on the sofa, his face lost in the cushions. His muffled voice could just be heard. "Has anyone checked the screens recently?" Even when he was half-asleep he could still ask important questions.

Nabster glanced up casually.

"Wha-what?" was all he managed to say, before shock set in.

Kennedy managed a bit more. "What is HAPPENING?!" she yelled. She tossed her diary to one side and leapt up from the table.

At that, Laurie's eyelids shot up like spring-loaded shutters.

Instead of the screen showing four images of a quiet entrance hall and donations container, one quarter showed a changing view with the picture rocking from side to side.

"How can it be moving?" Laurie asked exactly what the others were thinking.

The strange image came from the camera mounted on WeePal's shoulder. That meant WeePal was on the move.

"It doesn't make sense," said Nabster. "Zoe has gone home for the night."

"Or we thought she had," said Kennedy. "Who else could be controlling WeePal? Gus is away home too, isn't he?"

"Where is WeePal going?" asked Nabster.

"Let's run upstairs to watch." Kennedy's hand was already on the door handle. As usual, she was almost in the corridor before suggesting they leave.

"No!" insisted Laurie. "Let's not! We can watch what

WeePal is doing *and* where he's going from here, and if anyone is involved we won't interrupt them. If there's someone there who's *not* Zoe, they don't know they're being watched."

Kennedy looked suspiciously at Laurie, wondering whether he was just choosing the lazy sofa option. But he was right: they had a perfect view, even though they were many stairs and corridors away from the entrance hall.

The image from the little robot was slightly fuzzy and swayed from side to side, but they could tell he had climbed down from his pedestal.

"I feel a bit queasy," said Laurie, staring at the shaky picture.

"Maybe you should be lying down," said Nabster mockingly. "Oh, wait, you already are."

"Look! There he is!" Now the little robot appeared in the images from the two cameras fixed on the robotic arms over the doorway. They showed WeePal walking towards the donations container.

"What's he got in his hand?" asked Laurie. WeePal was holding a piece of string or wire with something hanging on the end of it.

"Looks like he's going fishing," said Nabster.

"I think that's *exactly* what he's going to do," said Kennedy, as they watched the little robot clamber up on top of the donations container.

"I don't believe it!"

"That robot is supposed to be helping us!"

"*WeePal* is the thief!"

Now the fourth image on the screen came alive.

The camera on the drain worm robot, which was buried in the pile of coins inside the container, showed WeePal's feet through the clear plastic. It also showed a wire with a magnet at the end dropping through the slot and slowly getting closer

and closer

and closer

before it connected with a coin. They watched as the little robot pulled the wire up and eased a coin out of the slot. Over the next ten minutes, many more were lifted in the same way. For the third night in a row, coins donated to the museum were shifting.

"Zoe has really tricked us," said Kennedy. "She *must* be up there out of sight controlling WeePal."

"But she helped set up the camera," said Laurie. "Why—?"

"Look! WeePal's off again!" interrupted Nabster. They all watched in tense silence as the camera on WeePal's shoulder showed him making his way out of the entrance hall, through the big museum hallways, towards The Robot Next Door exhibition.

But then he went right past the entrance...

"What...?"

...and turned right...

"Where...?"

...into the next room.

"Why...?

"Remind me what's in the room next to the robot exhibition...?" asked Laurie softly.

"You know," said Nabster. "We were there earlier."

"That's what this is all about!" cried Kennedy with certainty. "It's nothing to do with the donations container. That was just a practice run for... *the real crime.*"

The three Squad members all spoke together: "The million-pound coin in the claw!"

Chapter 8
In which Colin's clambering proves useful

"It's gold," said Nabster. "It won't stick. That million-pound coin is safe from magnets."

"Not when there's an iron claw wrapped around it," said Laurie.

"I can't believe we're standing here watching a crime taking place," said Kennedy. "And not just any crime! The theft of an exhibit worth a million pounds!" She was pacing up and down in frustration.

"But if we go now, we'll miss seeing what's happening.

It will be over before we get there," said Laurie.

They continued watching the wavering image from the camera on WeePal's shoulder. Inside the **Splash the Cash** exhibition, in gloomy light, the glass money box came into view.

They all gazed intently. The picture lurched about and then brass and glass filled that quarter of the screen. WeePal had clambered up onto the money box.

He was on top, looking down. Through the slot they could see the metal claw clasped around the million-pound coin.

And then...

... the screen turned to grey sparkly fuzz.

"NO-O-O-O!" shouted Nabster. "Not now!"

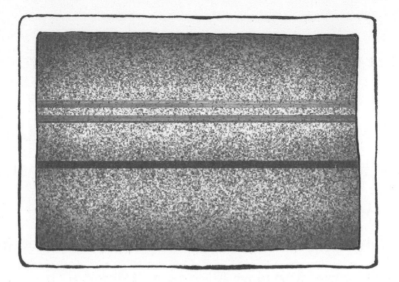

He dived for the laptop, his fingers rattling on the keys, trying every rescue function he knew to get the image back.

"Come on!" urged Laurie. "Fix it!!"

"I'm trying!" said Nabster, a deep frown on his face. "Nothing's working!"

Kennedy was hopping from one foot to the other. Her hands pulled at the ends of her hair.

"It's no good," said Nabster despairingly. "We've lost the connection."

"We need to get up there... NOW!" Kennedy turned to the door.

At that moment the image reappeared.

There was a moment of confusion as they all tried to make sense of what they were looking at.

This wasn't helped by the fact that the image was now on its side. They all tipped their heads.

"The camera has fallen off," said Nabster.

The screen showed the money box. There was nothing in it. And no sign of WeePal. The crime was complete.

In the cold light of day the next morning, down in the Squad's HQ, four things were very clear.

1. The coin in the claw, worth a million pounds, was missing.

2. WeePal was back on his pedestal in the entrance hall.

3. The Museum Mystery Squad had watched a crime being committed but had no idea who had done it.

4. Museum Director Magda Gaskar was not happy.

Gus had asked the Squad to go over and over and over again what they had seen on the screen the night before. Magda stood with her arms firmly folded. Each time the story was told, her frown deepened.

Zoe was brought down to the HQ for questioning. She seemed to be as confused as anyone, and was upset to hear that one of her robots had been involved in a major theft.

"It's honestly nothing to do with me," she said. "I got the bus home after I saw you. Someone else must have been controlling WeePal."

"Who else knows how to do it?" asked Laurie.

"Well, you three all do," she said. "Some of you were pretty good at it." She stared at Nabster.

It seemed that Zoe was viewing *them* just as suspiciously as they viewed *her*.

"Who can confirm that you were at home all evening?" asked Laurie.

"Er... no one," said Zoe. "Quiet night in. On my own."

There was an awkward silence.

"It's time to get the police involved." Magda was firm. "We've lost the centrepiece of an exhibition. I need this sorted out." The three Squad members looked worried as she reached for her phone.

The only noise was the plink and rattle of tiny claws on bars from Colin's side of the room. Nabster had taken his furry friend out and had been stroking him for comfort during the questioning. Then he'd placed Colin on top of the cage and the hamster was now picking his way across the bars, sniffing the air, as though enjoying the freedom.

"He likes it up there," said Nabster, trying to make conversation. "I think he's got a good head for heights."

Kennedy looked up. She had been twirling her hair in her fingers but she stopped like a statue with her hand in mid-twist.

"That's it! We shouldn't be looking *inside* the museum..." She was almost out of the door already. "Come on!"

Chapter 9
In which many stairs are climbed and a pen gets stuck

Frizzy ginger hair has its advantages. It was the one thing that helped Laurie and Nabster keep track of Kennedy as she ran through the crowds, even though they couldn't keep up with her. She was way in front of them, still shouting an occasional "Come on!"

Through umpteen corridors, round corners, up stairs...

"Where's she heading?" asked Laurie.

"Robot... exhib... ition..." panted Nabster breathlessly. Sure enough, in the distance they saw her disappear through the entrance to The Robot Next Door.

"Can we slow down? Please?" said Nabster. "We know where she is now." He ground to a halt, and bent over to recover. But a second later Kennedy burst back out into the corridor. She was holding something, but they couldn't see what.

"I hope you've got your breath back," said Laurie. "We're off again."

Nabster groaned.

They ran as best they could, following Kennedy to the staff stairwell. As they entered, Laurie shouted into the echoing space: "Kennedy... where are you going?"

"To the top!" came the reply.

Nabster gave Laurie a confused look. "What's up there?" he asked.

"The roof of course."

It was bright and cold outside as they stepped through

a door and onto the flat roof of the museum.

"Why have you brought us here?" panted Laurie. They had finally caught up with Kennedy. She was looking down through the glass panels in the roof, into the museum below. In her hand was a remote control.

"Colin's head for heights reminded me of someone else who enjoys being up high," she said. She pointed through the glass. Laurie and Nabster peered down at the robot room. It looked tiny below them. They saw the figure of Zoe at the tech desk. Even from a distance, they could tell by her movements that she was totally confused. Confused, because another figure was moving: WeePal. Kennedy was controlling the little robot from up on the roof. Zoe couldn't work out how the robot was walking when she wasn't operating it.

"Don the roofer said you get a great view of the birds and the rooftops from up here. And you do. But I think he had his binoculars pointing downwards."

"Spying on Zoe..." said Nabster.

"Learning how to control WeePal?" asked Laurie.

"Exactly," confirmed Kennedy.

Nabster reached for one of his new belt holders and pulled out his own binoculars. He walked around the glass roof panels, peering through. "You're right," he said. "It's a good view. And over here," he stepped across a low wall, "I'm above the next exhibition space. I can see the empty money box." He walked further across the roof. "And over here is the entrance hall and the donations container. Don could see everything."

"He just needed to whizz down on the rope to pinch the remote control and then he could use WeePal to do what he commanded from way up high. He practised robot coordination on the donations container and then did the real thing."

"You're absolutely right," said a voice.

It was Don the roofer.

He stepped out from behind the swinging stairwell door and continued talking while he opened a glass roof panel and adjusted his abseiling harness.

"Top marks for working it out. My advice next time: see if you can catch the person as well." He smiled and, still facing them, stepped backwards through the open panel.

WHIZZ BUZZZZZZZ

The wheels on the pulley system whirred and there was the familiar sound of gloves on rope as Don headed for the ground floor in record time.

"Quick! He's getting away!"

One glance showed that there was no quick way

down unless you were abseiling like Don.

Nabster's equipment didn't stretch to any mountaineering kit.

But he did have a shiny, sturdy metal pen. *And* it was easy to reach, in a newly made pocket on the outside of his sleeve – inspired by none other than Don himself.

Whipping the pen out like a quick-on-the-draw cowboy, Nabster jammed it into the abseiling pulley.

BUZZZzz— ZHT!

The noise of the gloves and clip running down the abseiling rope stopped as sharply as it had begun. The Squad peered over the edge of the open panel. Don was dangling in mid-air. His quick journey to the floor had been rudely interrupted. He was hanging over the robot exhibits, unable to go up or down.

There was a cry of rage as he looked back to the roof. The normally cheerful man was furious that he had been stopped. He was stuck high above the museum floor like a spider unable to make its silk thread any longer. He wriggled and writhed, adjusting his weight in the harness, trying to free the rope and re-start his descent.

"This might not hold for long," said Nabster, glancing at the jammed pen. It looked like it might crush to pieces under the stress of the rope and the weight of the roofer hanging below.

"Quick, let's get downstairs!" Kennedy dashed towards the stairwell door. Nabster followed. As he ran across the rooftop he grabbed the walkie-talkie hooked on his belt, called Gus and told him to go immediately to the robot exhibition. "Thanks for the ideas, Don," Nabster said, clipping the radio back in place. "That's twice in a minute your equipment-wearing ideas have helped us out!"

Kennedy and Nabster reached the stairs first and sped down. Their footsteps rattled like pipe-band drummers. Laurie went for the easier option:

sliding down the
banisters, casually
hopping off at each turn
of the stairs, and hopping
back on for the next
downward section. In his
silver shirt he looked like
a smoothly gliding robot.

They all arrived on the ground floor at the same moment, with Laurie looking less breathless and shaken after his smoother journey. Just as they reached the robot exhibition entrance, there was a familiar sound.

WHIZZ BUZZZZZZZ

Don was on the move again. Under pressure, Nabster's metal pen had snapped, freeing the rope. Broken shards of the pen fell with a tinkle to the museum floor.

"I knew that pen wouldn't last!"

"He's going to get away!"

"Quick!"

They burst into the exhibition, arriving beside Zoe's tech desk.

In the distance they saw that Don had landed on the ground. He was unclipping from the rope.

"Stop him!" shouted Kennedy, charging across the room.

Don gave her a steely look. He seemed to be struggling to free himself. Something had got tangled up.

"He's stuck!" cried Nabster.

"Quick! We can still catch him!" Laurie's voice was determined.

But instead of running like Kennedy, Nabster turned away from the action. He grabbed a remote control from the tech desk. With a flurry of fingers on buttons, a row of green lights flickered.

"What are you doing?" asked Laurie, perplexed. "There's no time for that."

But before he could say any more, a new figure began moving beside them. It didn't run, but it crossed the floor fast. It strode mechanically but silently, overtaking Kennedy and eating up the distance to the culprit.

It was BigPal.

Chapter 10
In which we see how helpful a robot can be

Expertly using the joystick, Nabster directed the big robot straight at Don the roofer. By now the red-headed man was almost free of the tangle. One last clip. He glanced up, aware that something was happening. The robot was almost on him. There was a moment of confusion as Don realised he was right in the way of this large marching machine.

Nabster's face was a picture of concentration. As BigPal reached the roofer, Nabster pulled a second joystick. The robot's arms rose like a lurching zombie, about to attack.

Don cried out and staggered backwards. He was free of the harness but the robot clattered right into him, knocking him to the ground.

"Pleased to meet you," said BigPal.

The stricken thief tried to get up again, but BigPal kept moving forward and knocking him back down.

"Pleased to meet you."

Three, four, five times it happened, but each time the roofer backed away and fell, he was getting nearer to a side door.

He glanced behind and saw how close he was to escaping the room and this unstoppable machine.

He turned and reached out for the door handle.

At that instant the door burst open, pushing him backwards, right into the mechanical arms of BigPal.

Gus had arrived.

"Pleased to meet you," said BigPal.

Five minutes later, the exhibition was a lot busier. The Squad, Zoe and Gus had been joined by Magda and the police, who were now dealing with Don.

BigPal stood silently, awaiting further instruction.

Nabster was apologising to Zoe for using an expensive bit of equipment without permission, although BigPal had accosted the thief without getting damaged.

"We'd never realised crime-fighting was one of his functions, but we'll have to think again," said Zoe.

"He was brilliant," said Nabster.

"Well, he's only as good as the person controlling him." Zoe was impressed with Nabster's skills. He looked away, embarrassed but proud.

"I want to congratulate you all," said Magda. "I asked

you to look at the mystery of a few coins on the floor and you managed to catch the man who stole one of the museum's most valuable items!"

"It's not often we get to film a crime taking place," said Kennedy. "Don didn't realise we'd put a camera onto WeePal."

"Cameras and robots," said Nabster. "Gadgets are the best solution to any problem!"

"Quite correct," said BigPal.

Last chapter
In which the case is closed

A day later, the Squad were back in their headquarters. The fuss had died down and everything was getting back to normal upstairs. The museum roof was fixed. The million-pound coin in the claw had been found in one of Don the roofer's many pockets and was back in the money box, waiting for the new **Splash the Cash** exhibition to open.

After the news coverage, The Robot Next Door exhibition was pulling in even bigger crowds keen to see WeePal, the thief helper, and BigPal, the thief catcher.

Lots of coins were being dropped into the donations container, and now they were staying there until Gus emptied it.

Things were pretty much as normal downstairs in the Museum Mystery Squad HQ too.

Colin was snoozing again. His new carrot-dispensing toy lay untouched in his cage. After pressing the buttons so much in the last couple of days he was tired and had a very full tummy. He was happily snoring. Just like Laurie.

Nabster didn't mind that his hamster invention was no longer in use. He had finished another new gadget.

"Here you go," he said to Kennedy, as he tightened the last screw.

"Let's give it a try," she replied, emptying her jar full of coins into a large funnel. They rattled down into the machine. A digital display on the front sped through numbers as it counted up her money.

Even though he had created another successful invention, there was one thing Nabster was missing.

"I still wish we had one of those robots in here," he said.

"Well, we do have Laurie dressed up as one instead," said Kennedy.

"The trouble is, he won't do anything. He just lies there, half-asleep."

"I might be half-asleep, but you know I'm still pretty useful," said a muffled voice from the sleeping bag.

"If Laurie *was* a robot, I know which button would be his favourite," said Nabster.

Kennedy grinned. "The off switch!"

"Night night," said their horizontal friend.

MONEY MONEY MONEY

The Squad have some money left over from their holidays. Can you find all the names of currencies in this money wordsearch?

DOLLAR (USA)	**RUPEE** (India)	**FRANC** (Switzerland)
YEN (Japan)	**BAHT** (Thailand)	**DINAR** (Iraq)
RAND (South Africa)	**POUND** (UK)	**PESO** (Argentina)
KRONE (Norway)	**EURO** (Europe)	**YUAN** (China)

A	S	D	R	T	E	A	P	S	E
P	D	F	Y	A	Z	S	R	T	T
S	D	I	E	M	N	G	U	E	A
P	R	A	N	A	P	B	P	O	M
P	A	D	T	A	E	R	E	M	R
A	L	R	H	U	R	P	E	S	O
B	L	N	R	A	N	D	T	I	S
H	O	L	C	Y	A	R	N	R	D
P	D	S	E	R	R	E	K	R	I
J	E	T	S	T	X	O	R	U	E
F	Y	E	H	D	O	W	O	P	A
R	E	A	N	P	N	A	N	E	L
A	B	Y	U	A	N	U	E	R	O
N	U	Z	E	R	P	S	O	R	T
C	A	N	A	H	A	R	Y	P	E

Answers at the back

Mike Nicholson

Mike Phillips

Mike Nicholson is a bike rider, shortbread baker, bad juggler and ear wiggler, and author of the *Museum Mystery Squad* series among other books for children.

Mike Phillips learnt to draw by copying characters from his favourite comics. Now he spends his days drawing astronauts, pirates, crocodiles and other cool things.

MUSEUM MYSTERY SQUAD

and the Case of the

Hidden Hieroglyphics

Mike Nicholson

A mysterious message hidden for thousands of years: can the Squad discover the mummy's secret before it unravels?

ANSWERS

MONEY MONEY MONEY
(Page 133)

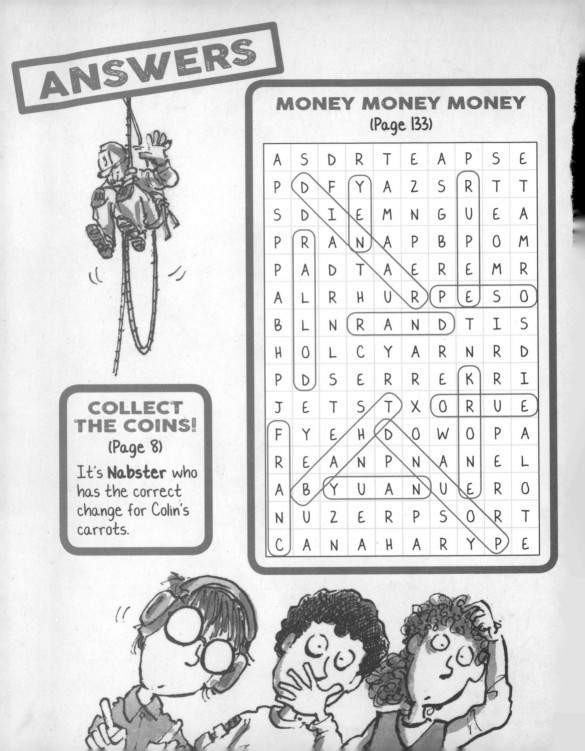

COLLECT THE COINS!
(Page 8)

It's **Nabster** who has the correct change for Colin's carrots.